BILLY AND THE MINI MONSTERS

Monsters in the Dark

ZANNA DAVIDSON

Illustrated by
MELANIE WILLIAMSON

Reading consultant: Alison Kelly

Contents

Gloop   Fang-Face   Captain Snott   Peep   Trumpet

Chapter 1
The Footprints

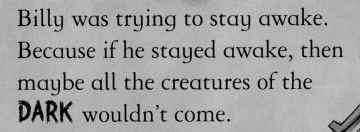

Billy was trying to stay awake.
Because if he stayed awake, then
maybe all the creatures of the
DARK wouldn't come.

3

Billy imagined all sorts of scary things that might gobble him up in the **DARK**.

Terrible trolls

Blood-sucking gizzlers

Shadow skulkers

Fang-busting zombies

But Billy's bed was very warm.
And his eyes kept closing by
mistake and then, finally...

Z
z
z Z
z Z Z z z Z
Z z z Z Z z

He fell fast asleep.

Z
z
z z Z z z Z
Z z Z z z Z z
z
z Z

As Billy slept...

Z
z

Pitter-patter

Pitter-patter

He woke suddenly.

Pitter-patter

What *was* that?

Pitter-patter

THUNK!

A loud noise made Billy reach for his torch. Then he heard a voice – a squeaky little voice.

Mmmm... Cheese!

Talking mice? Billy gulped. He
swung his torch beam around the
room. Nothing!
Then he saw his bookcase...

books
knocked
over

pot of
paint

pool of
purple paint

...and lots of tiny purple

FOOTPRINTS!

They didn't look like
mouse footprints.

What are
they?

Billy followed
the footprints…

They led to what had once been his
cheese sandwich. It had been…

…ATTACKED!

"Perhaps I'm dreaming," thought Billy. "I must be dreaming. I'll go back to bed and not think about scary creatures. And in the morning the footprints will be

ALL GONE..."

...won't they?

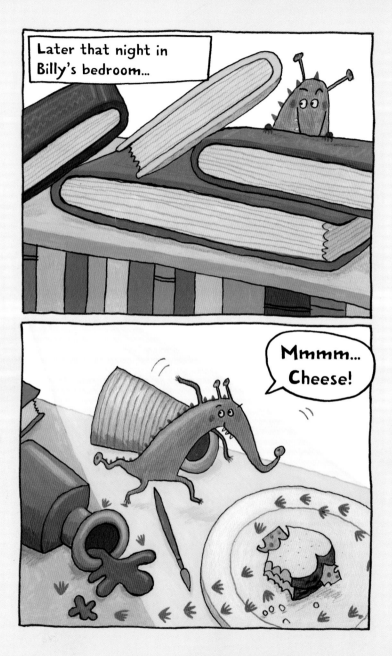

13

Chapter 2
The Sock Drawer

The next morning,
the footprints hadn't
gone. In fact, there were
more of them.

Billy raced downstairs.

"Something happened… in the night…" he said.

His family looked up from the breakfast table.

And now there are strange **purple** footprints all over **my** bookcase.

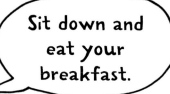

Sit down and eat your breakfast.

But...

"Silly Billy,"
said Ruby, Billy's
little sister.

"There really are!" cried Billy.
"Please! Come upstairs and see."

But when his parents opened
his bedroom door...

"I don't understand," said Billy.
The footprints had gone.

"Now, Billy," said his mum.
"You must stop making things…"
She paused… and sniffed…

"…YUCK!"

"I don't make things yuck!"
cried Billy.

"I mean that **revolting** smell,"
said his mum. "And it's coming
from your sock drawer."

It stank of rotting cheese and stale farts.

"It's not my fault!" said Billy.

It must be the chest of drawers. It's **Dad's** fault for buying it from that smelly old junk shop.

It didn't smell when I bought it, Billy.

"I'll sort it out later," sighed Billy's mum.

Come on, it's time to get dressed.

Billy quickly put on his uniform. Then he stood in front of the mirror to do his tie.

He froze.

There was a large bite-sized chunk missing from the end of his tie.

And something was moving in the corner of the mirror. It flashed past, a blur of purple fur and…

Were those HORNS?

He spun around, but whatever it was had gone…

Billy ran!

24

25

Chapter 3
Billy Makes a Plan

Billy was quiet on the way to school. He wanted to tell his mum about the purple furry **THING**, but she'd never believe him.

And she was still angry about his tie…

Did he *eat* his tie?

Please look after your tie!

Yes, Mum.

He was going to have to work this out for himself. Even if it took him the

rest
of his
life!

He decided to write a list.

Strange things that are happening in my bedroom

1. My new chest of drawers smells disgusting.

   (It's *NOT* my socks.)

2. There were purple footprints on my bookcase...

3. ...that mysteriously

disappeared!

4. There's something in my room that likes eating cheese... And ties.

5. It might be purple and furry... ...with HORNS!

6. And it's definitely VERY SCARY!

Maybe the **STRANGE** creature was living in his new chest of drawers?

Billy knew exactly what he was going to do. He was going to set a **trap**. Tonight!

Oh no! Trumpet's trying to find more cheese!

After him, Captain Snott!

37

Chapter 4
The Cheese Trap

Billy had finished his trap.

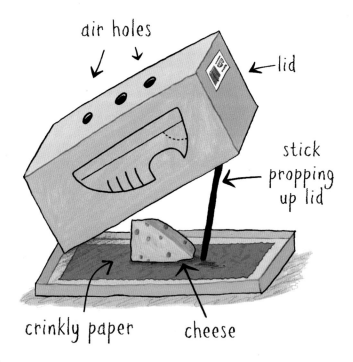

air holes

lid

stick propping up lid

crinkly paper

cheese

He'd made an **Action Plan** too.

Action Plan

1. Turn off lights. May need darkness for monster to come.

2. Try VERY hard not to be too scared of the scary dark.

3. Wait for sound of cheese-eater-creature on crinkly paper.

4. Slam down lid.

5. Trap the cheese-eater!

Mum and Dad had kissed
Billy goodnight. Now he was
under his duvet with his torch
and his notebook.

He was going to do this properly
and write everything down.

9pm Nothing. Very dark.

9.40pm Still very dark.
I think I fell asleep for a little bit...

9.55pm Nothing. The cheese is still there.

...Eeek!!

What's that?

Crickly-crackly noises?!
In the dark!

Billy reached for his torch.
There, against his wall, was an...

...ENORMOUS

MONSTER-
SHAPED
SHADOW

with

HUGE

spiky horns.

Billy tried to scream
but no sound came out.

In his panic, he dropped his
torch. It rolled off his bed

AND WENT OUT.

The shadow had gone but
there, glowing in the darkness,
was a monster.

It was green. It had horns.
Only it wasn't enormous.

It was...

it was...

tiny.

CRASH!

BANG!

Chapter 5
Slime

The monster
squeaked, and ran.
Billy dived after it…

…and missed. He switched on his torch and scanned the room.

Aha!

The monster was heading for the sock drawer!

A moment later, it had vanished.
Billy pulled open the drawer and
plunged his hand inside…

There was gloopy slime
EVERYWHERE!

Great globby clumps of
it, dripping off his drawer.
Huge globby lumps of
it all over his socks. And
underneath all the slime
there were more…

MONSTERS!

"But I always thought monsters were **BIG**," Billy blurted out.

"You're all so… er… mini!"

"WE ARE NOT MINI,"

snapped Captain Snott.
"*You* are ridiculously big."

"And we are
VERY scary,"
growled
Fang-Face.

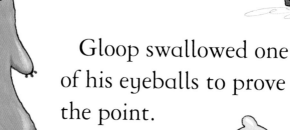

Gloop swallowed one
of his eyeballs to prove
the point.

It re-emerged a
few moments later
on his left leg.

We are
MONSTERS
of the dark.

Peep hissed and rose
up into the air.

Billy started to laugh.
He had **MONSTERS** in his room.
Only they weren't terrifying. They
were actually really... cute.

Suddenly, Billy's bedroom door swung open.

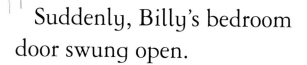

I heard some funny noises – why are you out of bed, Billy?

"It's been one thing after another today," his mum went on. "First stories of footprints, then your tie – and that smelly drawer!"

"It's time to sleep, otherwise you'll be tired in the morning. And I promise you there aren't any **MONSTERS** under your bed."

Billy's mum left.

Just then, there was a small

toot!

followed by a very stinky smell.

"What's that **WHIFF?**" thought Billy. Then he remembered his trap. He raced over and opened the lid.

A fart monster!

"You're the reason my sock drawer **STINKS!**" he whispered to the little monster.

The other monsters slowly
peered out from the sock drawer.

"That's Trumpet," sighed
Captain Snott.

"I don't always fart,"
said Trumpet.

Only when
I've eaten too
much cheese.

"But what are you doing here?"
asked Billy, carrying Trumpet over
to his chest of drawers.

"We live here," replied Captain
Snott. "The sock drawer is our home."

"**Billy!**" said his mum, coming back into the room. "What *is* going on? Why are you talking to your socks?"

"I'm not," said Billy, shutting the drawer as Trumpet dived for cover. His mum looked suspicious. She strode over and reached for the handle.

Don't open the drawer!

His mum opened the drawer.
"Don't touch the socks!"
cried Billy.

**His mum
touched
the
socks!**

"Urgh!"
she yelped.
"There's slime in here!
This is too disgusting.
I'm going to have
to deal with this

RIGHT NOW."

"**Wait!**" cried Billy.
"Where are you taking them?"
   "To the washing machine!"
replied his mum. "And there'll be
no TV for a week."

Then she left.

Billy looked
over at Trumpet.

A little tear slid
down Trumpet's face.
"I'll never see my friends again."

You have to
save them! Or
they'll drown!

Chapter 6
Billy to the Rescue

Billy opened his door onto the dark, dark hall.

"You will help them, won't you?" asked Trumpet.

Billy gulped.

He could hear his parents in their bedroom at the other end of the passage. He would be all alone in the dark downstairs.

ALL

ALONE

WITH GHOSTS

AND ZOMBIES

AND SKELETON

HANDS...

"The only thing is… it's very dark down there," said Billy. Trumpet crossed his arms and narrowed his eyes.

69

"I can do this," thought Billy.
"I can go downstairs in the dark."

SLOWLY,
HE
BEGAN
TO
CREEP
DOWN
THE
STAIRS.

The floorboards
creaked and groaned.
The wind whistled
and moaned.

The dark is nothing to be afraid of. Trust me. I'm a monster. I live in the dark.

Billy ran to the kitchen.
There were the Mini Monsters
tumbling around
in the machine.

Billy pressed button after
button. Beep! Beep! Beep!
He pulled open the washing
machine door and water, soggy
socks and four wet Mini
Monsters flooded out
onto the floor.

Billy looked at the mess
and groaned. He was going
to be in big trouble for this.
But there was no time
to clear it up.

Phew!
We're free!

He scooped up the Mini Monsters
and raced back to his room.

Billy tiptoed across the carpet and carefully placed the monsters in a comfy new drawer.

Thank you! In return for saving us, we offer you our Secret-Hairy-Snot-Tooth Oath of Devotion.

Er... thanks. What's that?

It means we will never leave you.

"You saved us," explained Gloop. "Now it's our turn to save you."

"We will come with you everywhere – to school, to the park…"

"But I don't need saving," protested Billy. "And since you've arrived, I've been in even **more** trouble than usual."

But the monsters weren't listening. They'd found some of Billy's T-shirts and were already settling back into their drawer.

Just then, Billy's dad
walked past his door.

Billy! You
need to go
to sleep!

Billy clicked off his light.
Then he grinned as he realized
something. There was no light in
his room but he didn't mind.

He wasn't scared of the dark any more!

A moment later, there was a small parp, followed by a terrible smell. Billy sat up in bed as five monsters emerged from the drawer.

TRUMPET!

And then came a louder cry from his dad.

Oh, Billy. Yuck! What a smell!

All about the
MINI MONSTERS

FANG-FACE

LIKES EATING:
socks, school ties,
paper, anything
that comes his way.

SPECIAL SKILL:
has massive fangs.

SCARE FACTOR:
9/10

GLOOP

LIKES EATING: cake.

SPECIAL SKILL:
very stre-e-e-e-tchy.
Gloop can also swallow
his own eyeballs and
make them reappear on
any part of his body.

SCARE FACTOR:
4/10

CAPTAIN SNOTT →

LIKES EATING: bogeys.

SPECIAL SKILL:
can glow in the dark.

SCARE FACTOR: 5/10

PEEP

LIKES EATING: very small flies.

SPECIAL SKILL: can fly (but not very far, or very well).

SCARE FACTOR: 0/10 (unless you're afraid of small hairy things)

TRUMPET →

LIKES EATING: cheese.

SPECIAL SKILL: amazingly powerful cheese-powered parps.

SCARE FACTOR: 7/10 (taking into account his parps)

Series editor: Becky Walker
Edited by Lesley Sims and Becky Walker
Designed by Reuben Barrance and Brenda Cole
Cover design by Hannah Cobley

Digital manipulation by John Russell

First published in 2017 by Usborne Publishing Ltd., Usborne House,
83-85 Saffron Hill, London EC1N 8RT, England. www.usborne.com
Copyright © 2017 Usborne Publishing Ltd. UKE